First published in Great Britain in 1999 by Bloomsbury Publishing Plc
38 Soho Square, London, W1V 5DF
This paperback edition first published 2000

Text copyright © Bernard Ashley 1999
Illustrations copyright © Anne Wilson 1999
The moral right of the author and illustrator has been asserted

A CIP catalogue record of this book is available from the British Library
ISBN 0 7475 4700 9 (paperback)
ISBN 0 7475 4149 3 (hardback)

Designed by Dawn Apperley

Printed and bound in Hong Kong / China by South China Printing Co.

3 5 7 9 10 8 6 4 2

THIS BLOOMSBURY BOOK

BELONGS TO

....

Growing Good

Bernard Ashley and Anne Wilson

BLOOMSBURY
CHILDREN'S
BOOKS

All his life Samuel had lived in the shadow of the box factory.
Each morning for four years he'd woken up to its brick walls.

Till one day the factory closed and they knocked it down. When the dust had settled over everyone's furniture, Samuel could look across the empty space. Now he could see Jade's flat, and Faustin's flat, and Arif's flat. And he could see the sun shining down instead of just shining on; and the rain falling from the sky instead of just running down the factory walls.

'So what's goin' in its place?' his Grandad Jess wanted to know when the planners came. 'We don't want nothin' taller!'
'No plans yet, we'll see what people want,' he was told.
'But it's got to make good use of the space.'

But Samuel enjoyed having the space with nothing on it.
It was a football pitch one day and a cycle track the next.
It was a firework display and a fairground. And then it was
just a space again.

One day when Samuel was going the quick way across to Jade's, he suddenly stopped and pointed to something he'd nearly trodden on.

'What's this, Grandad?' he shouted.

Peeping up through the dusty soil was something growing, a tendril, a plant taking a shy look at the world.

'Don't know what that is!' Grandad Jess said.

Samuel left the plant and ran on to play with Jade. But Grandad Jess kept it in his head – and when they got home he looked it up in a book. 'Old English Foxglove,' he told Samuel. 'That seed's slept there all these years, since before they built the factory. And with a bit of warm and a drop of wet, it's come to life again.'

He sat in his chair and told Samuel about the old plants of St Lucia: bananas and orchids and bamboo and hibiscus. He spoke with his eyes closed, and Samuel knew he was seeing pictures in his head of somewhere else altogether to here.

'Come on!' he said to Samuel next day, when Samuel's mother had gone to work. He took him out to where the foxglove was growing, and started measuring out the empty space. Samuel held the curly tape measure as Grandad Jess marked out the ground into plots. 'That gives everyone so much, with room for paths in between.'
'For what?' asked Samuel.
'For allotments,' said Grandad Jess. He put a rope round their own plot, and the two of them started digging the soil. Copying his grandad, Samuel pushed down with his foot, pulled up with his hands, and only stopped to watch the worms.

While they worked, people peeped and people peered, over their fences, through their windows, round their back doors. And, next day, Jade's grandmother was out roping a plot too, and digging it.

But Steve Tott from next door didn't want gardens. 'What we want here is somewhere to put our cars,' he growled. 'A decent car park.'
All the same, by the weekend there were ten different families out there forking and digging, trowelling and dibbing, firming-in and watering.

It wasn't long before the planners buzzed in like bees.
'Good use!' They wagged their fingers.
'What other plans you got?' Grandad Jess asked – as Samuel
carried a watering can to Jade's row of seeds, and Arif found
some string for Samuel's St Lucia beans.
'I've got plans!' declared Steve Tott, wanting to know how
soon a car park could be rolled out.

'There's no final decision till later this year,' the planners said.
'You'll know at the end of the summer.'
'So you can come back and see us then,' said Grandad Jess.
'When my fennel comes up I'll give you some to flavour your fish.'
'If you can find somewhere to park!' Steve Tott pushed in.

But week by week more people dug plots.
Grandad Jess drew up a plan and put it on his fence.
Steve Tott put up a paper for people to sign –
ALL WHO WANT A RESIDENTS' CAR PARK.

Samuel didn't notice any of that. His eyes were on the strip he'd planted with his seeds, watching for his St Lucia beans to start to climb. He watched, and watered, and when he thought he saw something which didn't belong, he weeded. And up the strings grew the beans, with another plant in the spaces between.

The spring went into summer, people all out there on their plots – old and young and in-betweens. There was laughing and music and the pronging of forks and lifting of spades. But never much shouting, except from Steve Tott if a bee came his way.

And still he went round the houses with his paper. When people weren't keen he told them how cars could get scratched in the road – after which some of them signed. Then Samuel helped Grandad Jess go round the allotments with a paper of their own. An invitation to run a charity day at the end of the season. And everyone they asked signed this paper.

Meanwhile plants started to grow all ways, too – helped by words of encouragement from the gardeners. And those plants must have understood. Because when the summer sunshine gave off its true warmth and the rain fell soft, the plants began to flourish.

Onion and okra and sorrel and spinach; and rhubarb and raspberry and lilac and lilies. Potatoes, pumpkin and poppies. Different leaves, different flowers, different colours, different uses: some for eating, some for seeing, some for smelling.

The planners came on the Charity Day. They looked at the old factory site, covered in green leaves and bright blooms and succulent fruits and pods. They looked at the growers in their colourful clothes as bright as the plants, and at the jazz band swinging up and down the paths between the plots. They put their heads in a huddle and shook them and nodded. Then they called Steve Tott over, and Grandad Jess.

'Well this looks like good use to us,' they said. 'And what people want.
What do you say, Mr. Tott?'
Steve Tott hadn't got many names on his paper. Some people with bright
flowers in their hair and hands had come to cross their names off. 'Erm,' he
said, 'let's see how it goes!'

The planners looked at Samuel's strip.
'And what have you got there, young man?'
Samuel told them. 'Beans from St Lucia.
And in between, old foxgloves,
from what was growing here before.'
'That's nice,' they said.

But Samuel wasn't listening. He was off with Jade,
dancing behind the jazz band in the allotment celebration.

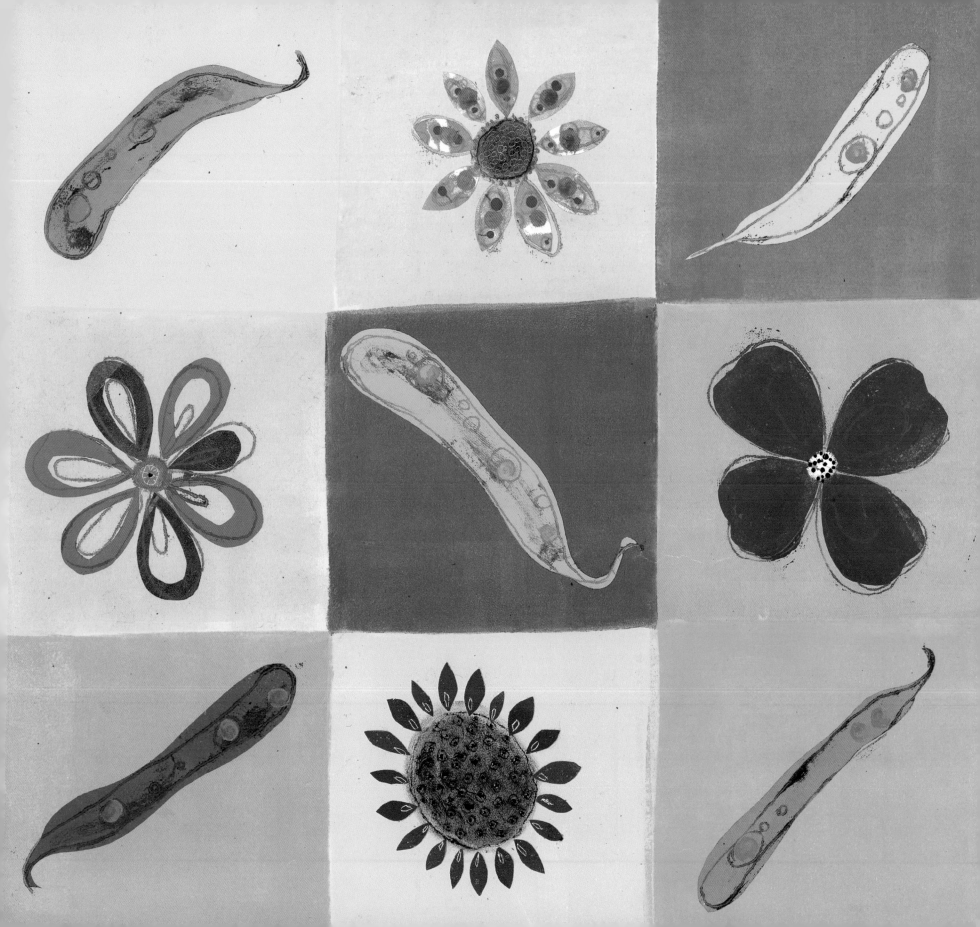

Acclaim for this book

'... Bernard Ashley's *Growing Good*, illustrated with éclat by newcomer
Anne Wilson, is utterly likeable: a joyous tale of the transformation of
a wasteland into a community garden (winning out over plans for a car park)
and is full of sunshine, dance and neighbourly love.' Nicolette Jones, *The Sunday Times*